KT-238-347

How to be a hero

This book is not like others you have read.
This is a choose-your-own-destiny book
where YOU are the hero of this adventure.

Each section of this book is numbered.
At the end of most sections, you will have
to make a choice. Each choice will take you
to a different section of the book.

If you choose correctly, you will succeed.
But be careful. If you make a bad choice,
you may have to start the adventure again.
If this happens, make sure you learn from
your mistake!

Go to the next page to start your
adventure. And remember, don't be a zero,
be a hero!

You are a captain in the Fairy Guard, living in the magical kingdom of Mab. The land is ruled by Gloriana, the greatest fairy queen that ever lived. Your duty is to protect her and the citizens of Mab.

In the land of Mab, dwarfs, fairies, giants and other magical peoples live together in peace. It is a land of happiness, but it also has its enemies who wish to destroy it.

The harmony that holds the kingdom together is created by the fairy rainbow, which is kept in a golden casket in the Ring of the Fairies. Once a day, the casket is opened, releasing the rainbow and spreading magic across the land. If the casket was ever lost or taken, the magic would fade away and the land of Mab would be no more.

Now go to 1.

CUMBRIA LIBRARIES

3 8003 04866 7281

I n

H E

YOUNG PEOPLES LIBRARY SERVICES

County Council

Libraries, books and more...........

"/19		

Please return/renew this item by the last date shown.
Library items may also be renewed by phone on
030 33 33 1234 (24hours) or via our website

www.cumbria.gov.uk/libraries

Cumbria Libraries

CLIC

Interactive Catalogue

Ask for a CLIC password

LONDON•SYDNEY

Franklin Watts
First published in Great Britain in 2019 by The Watts Publishing Group

Text © Steve Barlow and Steve Skidmore 2019
Illustrations by Judit Tondora © Franklin Watts 2019
The "2Steves" illustration by Paul Davidson
used by kind permission of Orchard Books

The authors and illustrator have asserted their rights in
accordance with the Copyright, Designs and Patents Act, 1988.

All rights reserved.

PB ISBN 978 1 4451 6969 9
ebook ISBN 978 1 4451 6971 2
Library ebook ISBN 978 1 4451 6970 5

1 3 5 7 9 10 8 6 4 2

Printed in Great Britain

MIX
Paper from
responsible sources
FSC
www.fsc.org
FSC® C104740

Franklin Watts
An imprint of
Hachette Children's Group
Part of The Watts Publishing Group
Carmelite House
50 Victoria Embankment
London EC4Y 0DZ

An Hachette UK Company
www.hachette.co.uk

www.franklinwatts.co.uk

1

One bright mid-summer morning you are in the stables grooming Aria, your kingfisher, when a herald appears at the door.

"Captain," she says, "the queen wishes to see you immediately at the Ring of the Fairies."

From the look on the herald's face, you know that something is very wrong.

To question the herald, go to 25.
To head to the Ring of the Fairies straight away, go to 36.

2

You turn and take hold of the casket but before you can fly away, Torkin grabs hold of you and pushes you towards the edge of the lava lake.

You try to break free of the elf's grip, but Torkin is too strong for you. You point your wand at the evil elf, but he brushes it away.

Your wand spins out of your hand and lands in the lake, where it burns to a crisp. Torkin snatches the casket from your grasp.

"You've failed, fairy," he shrieks. "I will rule the new land of darkness!"

Without your wand, you are powerless.

Torkin throws the casket into the lake of lava. It starts to melt.

You have failed and there's only one way to stop the rainbow being destroyed — start your quest again!

Go to 30.

3

You guide Aria down into a clearing in the forest.

"Stay here," you tell her. You pack more provisions and fly off through the trees. You hold out your wand to light up the way and fly as fast as you can.

Suddenly you come to a shuddering halt. You try to move but you can't. You're stuck in a giant spider's web!

Your wand and pouch of dust have fallen to the ground out of your reach.

The web starts to vibrate and you glance across to see a monstrous spider, jaws open, heading your way. You struggle desperately to free yourself, but it is hopeless. The spider closes in.

Go to 30.

4

You land in a field of flowers. You take your fairy knife, pierce a flower stem and drink the nectar as it oozes out. It is delicious! You continue to feast on the sweet liquid as the sun beats down.

You yawn and decide to lie down and rest before continuing.

Hours later you wake up to a cry of, "Captain!"

You look up to see another member of the Fairy Guard, riding her kingfisher. "You should not have fallen asleep!" she cries. "The magic rainbow has been destroyed!"

You know there is only one thing to do.

Go to 30.

5

"I am sorry," you cry, but the hobgoblin is in no mood for apologies!

He throws another boulder at you. You try to swerve to avoid it, but it hits you, sending you spinning out of your saddle and into the hobgoblin's hand. He tightens his grip, slowly squeezing the life out of you...

Go to 30.

6

You raise your wand, but an ogre's arrow hits it, sending it spinning from your hand!

To rescue your wand, go to 38.
To use your magic dust, go to 19.

7

"I can't tell you. It's a secret mission."
You turn towards the cloudberry bush.
"Very well, I won't tell you anything..."

If you wish to tell the sprite about Torkin, go to 31.
**To ignore the sprite and eat a
    cloudberry, go to 18.**

"What more do you know of Torkin?" you ask.

"He dwells in the Mountains of Fire near the Great Forest of the North. I believe that is where he is headed. I fear that he will throw the casket into the lava pits inside the mountain and destroy it. Find him and take back the casket before he can do this."

"I will do as you command," you reply.

"To help you in your quest, I have something for you."

The queen hands you a bracelet made from precious gemstones, all the colours of the rainbow.

"This is the Rainbow Bracelet. If you find yourself in deadly peril, place your hand on it, say, 'Rainbow take me home!' and you will return to this time and place. Now go — time is running out!"

To head to the Mountains of Fire immediately, go to 16.

To head back to the stables, to fly off on your kingfisher, go to 42.

9

As Torkin moves towards you, you point your wand at the golden casket and cry out, "Rainbow, help me!"

The casket's lid springs open and the rainbow streams out, filling the cavern with vivid red, orange, yellow, green, blue, indigo and violet light. The elf is swept up by the rainbow.

"Stop it!" he pleads. "I promise I'll be good!"

"Too much talking, Torkin!" you laugh. "Your powers might be more than mine, but the magic of the rainbow is the greatest power of all!"

There is a crash of thunder and Torkin vanishes. Then, as suddenly as it appeared, the rainbow retreats into the golden casket and the lid slams shut!

You pick up the casket and fly back to Aria, ready to head home.

Go to 50.

10

You continue your journey. Just as the sun is beginning to set, you glimpse the Great Forest of Mab and beyond that, the Mountains of Fire. A red glow from the mountains lights up the sky.

It has been a hard journey and you know that Aria needs to rest.

To head for the mountains, go to 23.
To land and rest in the forest, go to 40.

11

You fly around for hours, searching for some clue as to where you might find Torkin.

Suddenly there is a crash of thunder. A vast rainbow appears, momentarily lighting up the sky before it disappears, leaving only blackness and silence.

You realise that Torkin must have destroyed the casket and the rainbow.

You have failed.

Go to 30.

12

You take out your wand, point it at the oncoming swarm and cry, "Begone!"

A stream of stars pours from the wand, shooting across the sky and engulfing the hornets. An explosion of colour fills the air and the deadly creatures vanish.

A wave of relief sweeps across your body. That was close!

To land and get your strength back, go to 4.

To continue your journey, go to 45.

13

You say your farewells, mount Aria and head north.

The sun is setting as you approach the Mountains of Fire. As you get closer, you see a figure hurrying along one of the mountain tracks.

Is this Torkin? you wonder.

To follow the figure, go to 35.
To attack the figure, go to 24.

14

"We have no time to help. We must find the elf," you tell Aria. But before you can fly on, the air is filled with arrows. The ogres have seen you!

Aria gives a cry as an arrow pierces her wing. She spirals earthwards towards the waiting ogres.

To use the Rainbow Bracelet, go to 30.
To use the magic dust, go to 49.

You point your wand at the firewall and cry, "Begone!"

The fire instantly dies away, opening up a tunnel into the mountain.

Leaving Aria, you fly down the tunnel and reach a lake of molten lava. In the centre of the bubbling lake is a small, rocky island. On the island you see the golden casket sitting on a marble plinth.

To take the casket, go to 22.
To look for Torkin, go to 34.

16

With a flick of your wings you take to the sky and fly northwards towards the Mountains of Fire. You know you have to get there quickly, so you fly as fast as you can.

However, you are soon tired. You realise that you should have packed food and drink to help you on your journey.

To fly back and get your kingfisher, go to 42.

To land and find food, go to 4.

17

You spur Aria through the waterfall, but the power of the water is too great and you plummet into the pool.

Before you can swim to the side of the pool, you feel a tentacle wrap around your leg. Desperately you try to break free, but whatever this creature is beneath the water is too strong for you.

Go to 30.

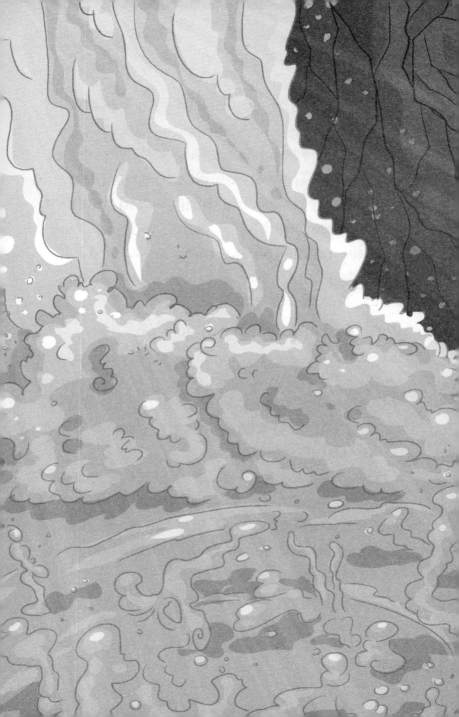

18

You pick a berry, pop it into your mouth and swallow it.

"You'll be sorry you did that!" the voice rings out. "They aren't cloudberries, they are dreamberries. You are going to sleep for a very long time!"

Suddenly you start to feel woozy. Your body becomes heavy and you drop to the floor. This is not good!

Go to 30.

19

You reach into your pouch, take a handful of dust and cast it towards the ogres.

"Be still!" you cry.

The dust covers the ogres and they come to a sudden halt, unable to move. They growl and curse at you, but can do nothing.

The stag wheels around. "Thank you," he says. "What brings you here?"

You tell him of your quest.

"I may be able to help you," he says.

"Some days ago, Torkin passed by and dropped this." He swishes his head and you see a silver key hanging on his antlers.

"Take it. It may help you find the way…"

You take the key.

"Goodbye and thank you again," you say.

With a flick of his head, he gallops away.

You make sure your wand is stored safely and decide what to do next…

To find somewhere to rest, go to 4.
To carry on to the mountains, go to 10.

20

As the elf runs at you, you sprinkle the ground with magical dust. A circle of shimmering white light surrounds you and the plinth.

Torkin crashes into it and falls to the floor. He picks himself up and snarls.

"You can't stay there forever. The dust's magic will wear off and then I will have the casket and the rainbow. I told you — in my realm, my power is greater than yours!"

He is right. The magic dust begins to lose its power and your protective circle fades.

To take the casket and flee, go to 2.
To open the casket, go to 9.
To use the Rainbow Bracelet, go to 30.

21

"Fly as fast as you can, Aria," you tell your kingfisher. She obeys at once and swings away from the swarm. However, the hornets are too fast.

You reach for your wand, but it is too

late. The swarm hits. Aria shrills in pain as she is stung over and over again by the deadly creatures.

You only have one way out of this!

Go to 30.

22

You fly over the bubbling lava towards the casket, but the lake erupts and a net of fire shoots up, trapping you in its fiery grasp.

Your wand bursts into flame, causing you to drop it into the boiling lava below. You are helpless!

Go to 30.

23

You decide to head for the mountains. Aria flies on, but she is slowing down.

You realise that you will have to land and rest for a short time or go on by yourself.

If you wish to rest, go to 40.
If you wish to carry on alone, go to 3.

24

You order Aria to speed at the figure. You aim your wand.

"Be still!" you cry. A stream of stars hits the figure but has no effect.

The figure turns — it is a hobgoblin.

They are immune to fairy magic and a lot bigger than an elf!

"Attack me would you, fairy? Pay for that you will!" It aims a huge boulder at you!

To apologise to the hobgoblin, go to 5.
To fly away, go to 48.

25

"Why does the queen wish to see me?" you ask.

"That is for her to say, not me," the herald replies. "She wishes to see you immediately, so the less you talk, the sooner you will be at the Ring of the Fairies."

You realise that the herald is not going to tell you anything more.

Go to 36.

26

You point your wand at the elf.

"Be still!" you command. The stars surround Torkin, but he breaks free!

"You are in my realm, fairy," he snarls. "My power is stronger than yours!" He runs towards the casket.

To fly to the casket, go to 22.

To try and stop Torkin reaching the casket, go to 46.

"Where are you?" you ask.

The voice calls out, "On the oak tree!"

You head over to the tree and see a small face sticking out of the bark. "A wood sprite!" you exclaim.

"What brings you here?" asks the sprite.

To tell the wood sprite about your mission, go to 31.

To keep it secret, go to 7.

28

As the swarm gets nearer, you reach into your pouch and take out a handful of magical dust. You fling the glittery particles towards the oncoming hornets, but the wind just blows them back into your face!

To try and out-fly the hornets, go to 21.
To use your wand, go to 12.

29

You point your wand and cry, "Be still!"

The salamanders are engulfed in a whirlpool of stars, transforming them into statues.

Heading to the stone door you take out the silver key the white stag gave you, place it into the lock and turn it. The door groans opens to reveal a long corridor. The walls glow with the heat from the mountain's lava. Ahead of you is a wall of flickering flames blocking the way.

To try and get past it, go to 15.
To find another way into the mountain, go to 39.

You grasp hold of the Rainbow Bracelet and cry out, "Rainbow, take me home!"

There is an explosion of colour and you find yourself back in the Ring of the Fairies.

Queen Gloriana stares at you. "You made a wrong choice. Begin your quest again and choose more carefully next time."

To head to the Mountains of Fire immediately, go to 16.

To head back to the stables to get your kingfisher, go to 42.

"I am hungry. First I will eat some cloudberries, then I will tell you what you wish to know."

The sprite speaks, "Don't! They aren't cloudberries — they're dreamberries! You'll sleep for days if you eat one!"

"Thanks for warning me," you say, and so you begin to tell the sprite about Torkin.

"I've never liked that elf," snarls the sprite. "He passed through here only this morning. He was heading for the Mountains of Fire."

Your heart leaps — you're on the right path and not far behind him. "Thank you. I must leave immediately."

"But I have more to tell," says the sprite.

If you wish to listen, go to 44.

If you want to hurry on after Torkin, go to 13.

32

Remembering what the sprite told you, you search for a waterfall.

Soon you see it crashing down the side of a mountain into a huge pool. You know the stone door is on the other side of the water...

To fly through the waterfall, go to 17.
To use magic on it, go to 41.

33

You guide Aria towards the fleeing stag. The ogres are closing in! Their grunts and cries fill the air.

You fly alongside the stag. "I will help," you tell the creature. "Gallop as fast as you can!"

The stag obeys as you spin Aria around to face the oncoming ogres. The foul creatures growl and sprint towards you.

To use your wand, go to 6.
To use your magical dust, go to 19.

You wonder why the casket is just sitting there on the plinth — *is it a trap?*

You decide to find Torkin. You hold out your wand and cry, "Reveal!"

A stream of stars shoots from the wand and dances through the cavern, searching for the elf. The stars spin around a large rock on the island.

"I know you are there, elf," you cry. "Show yourself!"

Torkin emerges from behind it. He sees you and laughs.

"I thought the queen would send someone to find me! I want you to see what I'm going to do and tell her how I destroyed the rainbow!"

He runs towards the casket.

To try and grab the casket first, go to 22.

To stop Torkin reaching the casket, go to 26.

35

You guide Aria towards the figure as it lumbers along the mountain track. As you get closer, you can see that it isn't an elf.

To question the figure, go to 24.
To fly away, go to 48.

36

You hurry to the Fairy Ring, where Queen Gloriana is waiting for you.

"Captain, I have terrible news," she says. "The golden casket has been stolen and, with it, the rainbow that keeps our kingdom safe."

You are shocked. "Who has taken the casket?" you ask.

"An elf called Torkin. He arrived here pretending to be sick. While my attendants were gathering herbs to cure him, he stole into this place and took the casket. He must be a creature of darkness and so, must hate the rainbow and its light. I need you to find the elf and return the casket before the magic of the rainbow is gone and our land is destroyed forever."

"But why don't you send all of your guards to rescue the casket?" you say.

The queen shakes her head. "This is a task for a hunter, not an army. One good fairy will succeed where many would fail."

To search for the elf immediately, go to 47.

To find out more about the elf, go to 8.

37

Just as the salamanders belch out their fireballs, you reach into your bag and throw the fairy dust. The dust transforms into water and the fireballs evaporate.

But there is no time to celebrate. The salamanders open their mouths again, once more revealing the glow of fire.

To use your wand against them, go to 29.

To continue to use the dust, go to 43.

38

You pull hard on your reins and spin Aria around. You see the wand lying on the ground and fly towards it. But you are too slow! An ogre snatches it up and snaps it in two.

You feel your heart miss a beat. Without your wand you know you have lost most of your magical powers. The ogres move in on you.

Go to 30.

39

You decide the firewall is impenetrable, so you turn and leap onto Aria's back before heading out of the cavern to search for another way into Torkin's realm.

Go to 11.

40

You guide Aria down to a forest clearing and make camp. At the edge of the clearing is a bush covered in bright-orange berries.

"Cloudberries!" you smile. You go to pick one.

Suddenly a voice calls out, "What do you think you're doing?"

Startled, you look around but can see nobody.

If you wish to ignore the voice and eat a berry, go to 18.

To try and discover where the voice is coming from, go to 27.

41

You spur Aria towards the waterfall, point your wand and cry, "Divide!"

The waterfall parts in two and you fly into a dark stone cavern.

You throw some of your magic dust into the air and the cavern lights up, revealing a huge stone door ahead. Two salamanders — fire dragons — guard the door. They turn their heads towards you and open their fire-drenched jaws.

To use your wand on these creatures, go to 29.

To use the fairy dust, go to 37.

42

You fly to the stables where Aria is waiting for you.

You pack your wand, a bag of fairy dust and provisions for the journey and are soon flying northwards.

As you urge Aria on, the air is suddenly filled with a horrendous buzzing. Ahead of you, the sky darkens and you let out a cry. A swarm of deadly giant hornets is flying towards you!

To try and out-fly the hornets, go to 21.
To use your wand, go to 12.
To use your magical dust, go to 28.

43

You throw the dust again and once more the flames turn into water.

However, the salamanders keep up their attack. You reach into your pouch for more dust — it is empty!

A fireball heads towards you...

Go to 30.

44

"What more do you know?" you ask.

"The entrance to Torkin's home in the mountains is through a stone door, hidden by a waterfall. But you will need a silver key to gain access."

You smile. "I have such a key!"

The sprite smiles. "Then you may be able to save the kingdom," it replies.

Go to 13.

45

You know there is no time to rest, so you urge Aria onwards.

As you skim across the grass meadows, you see a beautiful white stag being chased by a group of ogres armed with bows and arrows.

To fly on, go to 14.
To help the stag, go to 33.

46

You reach into your pouch and take out a handful of fairy dust. As you fly across the lake, you sprinkle it on the bubbling lava to stop it spitting up at you.

You speed towards the island and before Torkin can grasp hold of the casket, you land between him and the plinth.

"You can't stop me, fairy!" he screams. "I will destroy your rainbow and your kingdom!" He rushes at you.

To grab the casket, go to 2.
To avoid Torkin's attack, go to 20.

47

"I will set off immediately and find this elf. You have my word."

The queen shakes her head. "I appreciate your sense of duty, but you need to know more about Torkin before you depart."

You realise the queen is right.

Go to 8.

48

You order Aria to spin around and fly away. You have no time to waste and your grievance is with Torkin alone.

If the sprite told you about the waterfall, go to 32.

If it didn't, go to 11.

49

You reach into your bag, take a handful of magic dust and throw it over Aria's wing.

"Heal!" you cry.

The magical dust glistens and the kingfisher's wound mends instantly. With a beat of her wings, she pulls up away from the ogres, who turn their attention back to the stag.

"We have to do something to save the stag from those foul creatures," you tell Aria.

Go to 33.

50

Back in the Fairy Ring you hand over the casket to Queen Gloriana and tell her the story of your quest.

"Well done, Captain," she says. "I knew I could rely on you."

"But where has Torkin gone?" you ask.

"To the end of the rainbow," she replies. "I don't think we'll be seeing him again. You saved the kingdom. You are a real hero!"

Immortals

I HERO Quiz

Test yourself with this special quiz. It has been designed to see how much you remember about the book you've just read. Can you get all five answers right?

Question 1

Where do you meet Queen Gloriana at the start of the adventure?

A   the Western Forest

B   the Ring of the Fairies

C   the Ring of Fire

D   the Land of Elves

Question 2

What has Torkin stolen?

A   the golden casket and the kingdom's protective rainbow

B   the rainbow bracelet

C   the queen's magic

D   a fairy herald

Question 3

What type of bird do you fly?

A   a rook

B   a kingfisher

C   an owl

D   a robin

Question 4

Why does Torkin want the golden casket and its magical rainbow?

A   to capture the fairy queen

B   to kill the fairy queen

C   to turn all the fairies into elves

D   to destroy the rainbow and rule the new land of darkness

Question 5

Where has Torkin gone at the end of your adventure?

A   the Ring of Fire

B   the end of the rainbow

C   the land of darkness

D   the Mountains of Fire

About the 2Steves

"The 2Steves" are one of Britain's most popular writing double acts for young people, specialising in comedy and adventure. They perform regularly in schools and libraries, and at festivals, taking the power of words and story to audiences of all ages.

Together they have written many books, including the *Monster Hunter* series. Find out what they've been up to at:
www.the2steves.net

About the illustrator: Judit Tondora

Judit Tondora was born in Miskolc, Hungary and now works from her countryside studio. Judit's artwork has appeared in books, comics, posters and on commercial design projects.

To find out more about her work, visit:
www.astound.us/publishing/artists/ judit-tondora

Have you completed these I HERO adventures?

Battle with monsters in Monster Hunter:

978 1 4451 5878 5 pb
978 1 4451 5876 1 ebook

978 1 4451 5935 5 pb
978 1 4451 5933 1 ebook

978 1 4451 5936 2 pb
978 1 4451 5937 9 ebook

978 1 4451 5939 3 pb
978 1 4451 5940 9 ebook

978 1 4451 5942 3 pb
978 1 4451 5943 0 ebook

978 1 4451 5945 4 pb
978 1 4451 5946 1 ebook

Defeat all the baddies in Toons:

978 1 4451 5930 0 pb
978 1 4451 5931 7 ebook

978 1 4451 5921 8 pb
978 1 4451 5922 5 ebook

978 1 4451 5924 9 pb
978 1 4451 5925 6 ebook

978 1 4451 5918 8 pb
978 1 4451 5919 5 ebook

Also by the 2Steves...

978 1 4451 5885 0

Tip can't believe his luck when he
mysteriously wins tickets to see
his favourite team in the cup final.
But there's a surprise in store ...

978 1 4451 5892 1

Big baddie Mr Butt Hedd is in
hot pursuit of the space cadets and has
tracked them down for Lord Evil. But
can Jet, Tip and Boo Hoo find a way to
escape in a cunning disguise?

978 1 4451 5988 1

Jet and Tip get a new command
from Master Control to intercept
some precious cargo. It's time to
become space pirates!

978 1 4451 5979 9

The goodies intercept a distress
signal and race to the rescue. Then
some 8-legged fiends appear ...
Tip and Jet realise it's a trap!